Zippy the Runner

Written by Ji-yu Kim

Illustrated by Jeong-hyeon Seon

Edited by Joy Cowley

Zippy was a zebra who liked to run.
His body was skinny
and his legs were short,
but that didn't matter.
He still loved to run races.

Zippy never missed a race.

If he had a cold, he would run.

If his leg was sore, he would run.

He ran in the wind

and he ran in the rain.

But the results were always the same.

PAPPA GALLO

Zippy always finished last.
His friends used to say,
"It's okay. You did your best."

But when Zippy kept losing,
his friends said to him,
"Maybe running is not for you.
Why don't you take up painting?"

However, Zippy did not stop running.
When he finished last for the hundredth time,
his friends said, "Why do you still run?
Why don't you give it up?"

"I love running," Zippy told them.
"Even when I'm last, I love it."

Zippy did stretches,
drank some healthy spinach juice,
and then did some running practice.

As he ran around the path,
he saw Winnie the pig
sitting under a tree.
"You look sad," said Zippy.

"I am sad," said Winnie.
"I have never won a race.
You always come in last
so why do you still practise?"

Zippy said, "I might be last now,
but I hope I can do better next time."

"What if you are last next time?"
asked Winnie the pig.

"There is always another next time,"
said Zippy. "The sun sets
and the sun rises again.
Hope is like the sun."

That night, under the moon,
Zippy and Winnie ran and ran
along the practice path.

The next time there was a race,
the friends said to each other,
"Good luck! Happy running!"

Bang!
The starting gun went off
and the animals ran like the wind,
kicking up clouds of dust.

Winnie crossed the finish line.
He was not first. He was not last.
He was in the middle.
And that was better
than he had ever done before.

But Zippy was in last place again.

21

When Zippy crossed the finish line,
his friends clapped and cheered.
"Zippy never gives up
even though he is last.
Zippy gives us all hope."

After that, Zippy's friends
began the **HOPE** running team.

Zippy runs with his friends
because he loves running
more than anything in the world.
He also wants to bring hope
to all those who finish last.

Dear Zippy,

Thank you for letting me practise my running
with you. I was ready to give up running.
You showed me how to keep trying.
I learned I should never give up
on something I love to do.
I will keep trying because I might be able
to do better next time. You give me hope!

Your friend,
Winnie the pig

big & SMALL

Original Korean text by Ji-yu Kim
Illustrations by Jeong-hyeon Seon
Original Korean edition © Aram Publishing

This English edition published by big & SMALL
by arrangement with Aram Publishing
English text edited by Joy Cowley
Additional editing by Mary Lindeen
Artwork for this edition produced
in cooperation with Norwood House Press, U.S.A.
English edition © big & SMALL 2015

ISBN: 978-1-925233-89-6

Printed in Korea